# a funny sort of DOG

First published in Great Britain 1997 by Heinemann and Mammoth,
imprints of Reed International Books Ltd
Michelin House,  81 Fulham Rd, London, SW3 6RB
and Auckland and Melbourne

10 9 8 7 6 5 4 3

Text copyright © Elizabeth Laird 1997
Illustrations copyright © Russell Ayto 1997

The author has asserted her moral rights
The illustrator has asserted his moral rights

Paperback ISBN 0 7497 3114 1
Hardback ISBN 0 434 97368 8

A CIP catalogue record for this title is available
from the British Library

Printed at Oriental Press, Dubai, U.A.E.

# a funny sort of DOG

Elizabeth Laird • Illustrated by Russell Ayto

🍌 YELLOW BANANAS

# Chapter One

'HEY, LOOK WHO'S here! It's him again! It's Simon!'

Simon looked round desperately for somewhere to hide. It was hopeless. The lane was long and edged with steep banks on either side. He'd never make it to the main road that led to the school before Lennie got him.

'Looking for your uncle, are you, Simon? The one that kills sharks with his bare hands?'

Simon's heart was pumping. It had been a mistake making up that stuff about Uncle

Pete, who was just an ordinary sailor and never killed anything. Lennie hadn't believed him for a moment.

Lennie was circling round him, looking like a hungry shark himself. Suddenly, he nipped in and pulled at Simon's bag. It flopped open and his lunch box fell out.

'Oh, look! A Mars Bar! You don't like Mars Bars, do you, Simon? You'd like me to have it, wouldn't you, Simon?'

Simon nodded miserably. He was wishing and wishing and wishing that something would happen, that a hurricane would blow Lennie away, or that a Tyrannosaurus rex would jump out from behind Mrs Stafford's privet hedge and eat him.

Then, for the first time ever, something did happen.

'Hello Simon. Come and see what I've got!'

A big heavy man, brown from months at sea, with a pack on his back and tattoos on his hands, was actually coming up the lane.

'Uncle Pete!' shouted Simon.

Lennie dashed off at once, and he even dropped the Mars Bar back into Simon's box first.

'That kid give you any hassle?' said Uncle Pete, frowning at Lennie's disappearing back.

'No,' lied Simon. He'd forgotten Lennie already. He was looking at the animal trotting along beside Uncle Pete on the end of a lead.

'That's not . . .' he said.

'Yes, it is,' said Uncle Pete. 'It's for you. Your new dog. I wrote and asked your mum if you could have one, and she said it would be OK.'

Simon squatted down and patted the rough fur between the dog's funny round ears. He was surprised.

He'd expected their new dog to be a
spaniel, like poor Tracker, who'd got
really ill and been put down three
months ago. But this dog was
bigger than Tracker already, and he
looked odd. His legs were short and his
paws were huge. His ears were as
round as furry saucers and there was
a dark tip to his long pale tail.

'What kind of dog is he then?' he said. 'He looks more like a . . .'

'Blessed if I know,' Uncle Pete interrupted. 'I got him cheap from a man at the dock because he doesn't bark. Funny old geezer he was. Seemed in a terrible hurry to sell.'

The dog licked Simon's hand. He had a rough, rasping tongue, not a bit like Tracker's which had been soft and slobbery. Then he tapped at the end of Simon's blue scarf. His sharp claw caught in the wool and the scarf fell off Simon's neck. The dog began to play with it, jumping on it and buffeting it with his paws.

'He's lovely. I really, really like him,' said Simon.

'I hope your mum does,' said Uncle Pete anxiously.

Simon did not answer. He knew what Mum would do. She'd make a fuss, and say it was just like Pete to get her a guard dog that couldn't bark, and she'd never ask him to do anything for her ever again, and then she'd get all keen on the new dog and everything would be all right.

At least, he hoped it would. He'd got all keen on the dog already. Extremely keen. Desperately keen.

He bent down and tickled the puppy under its furry chin. The puppy's tail lashed from side to side and the dark tip caught Simon on the nose. 'Tip,' he said. 'That's what I'll call you, Tip.'

From down the road a bell rang.

'Better hop off to school, then, Simon,' said Uncle Pete. 'Don't worry, he'll be waiting for you when you get home.'

# Chapter Two

SIMON THOUGHT ABOUT the new dog all day long, all the way through assembly and English and P.E. He thought about him at break and at lunch-time, and while he was drawing a picture for his project on wildlife in Africa.

The minute the bell went at the end of the afternoon, Simon tore his jacket off its peg, grabbed his bag and dashed through the swing doors, nearly knocking Miss Parker off her feet.

He was home in ten minutes flat.

His mum was in the kitchen.

'Where is he?' panted Simon. 'Where's Tip?'

'Is that what you're going to call him?'
Mum didn't sound too pleased. 'He's in the
sitting room.'

Simon looked at her anxiously.

'Don't you like him, Mum?'

'Oh, I like him, all right,' she said doubtfully. 'He's very nice. It's just that . . .'

The door was nudged open and Tip came in. Simon dropped onto his knees.

'Here, Tip! Good dog! Come here!'

Tip ignored him. He'd suddenly spotted a fly, and was sitting back on his haunches, patting at it with his paws.

Simon roared with laughter.

'Go on, Tip! Catch it! Isn't he great, Mum?'

His mum was frowning.

'I've never seen a dog do that before.'

'That's because he's special. Brilliant, aren't you, Tip?'

Tip had forgotten the fly, and was busy licking his foreleg. Simon reached out a hand to stroke his tummy.

'Careful,' his mum said sharply. 'He's got wicked little teeth, I can tell you. Gave me quite a nip this morning. And his claws are amazingly sharp too.'

'A bit like a cat's,' said Simon.

'Exactly,' said his mum, and she went out of the kitchen and closed the door with a snap.

# Chapter Three

THE REST OF that term was Simon's best
ever. One reason was that Lennie had
disappeared. He'd probably gone off to
Chicago to train as a real gangster,
Simon thought.

Things were going better at school too.
People had always seemed to tease Simon
and gang up on him, but now, for the first
time, they were leaving him alone. One boy,
James, was even being quite friendly.

But best of all was Tip. Every moment when
he wasn't at school, Simon played with Tip,

and talked to Tip, and fed Tip and ran with Tip round and round the garden, trailing his blue scarf, which was now torn and tattered, for Tip to pounce on.

And Tip grew. He ate and he grew. He grew and he ate.

After a while, Simon stopped taking Tip out for walks. People made too many remarks.

'Funny sort of dog, that,' they'd say. 'Never seen one like him before. What sort of breed would you say he is?'

Then there
was the awful day he'd
taken Tip to the green in the middle of
the village. Tip had seen a squirrel, and had
somehow slipped off his lead and actually
chased the squirrel up a tree in the recreation
ground.

Quite a few people had stopped and
said things.

'Good heavens! Fancy a dog climbing a tree!'

'Doesn't look like a dog to me. More like a cat, really.'

'Bit big for a cat, unless it's a . . . No! It couldn't be!'

'The keeper won't like this, young man. He's too heavy for that branch. It'll break in a minute. You'd better get him down.'

Simon got used to keeping Tip at home, out of the way.

Then, one day, Lennie was back. He was lying in wait for Simon at the end of the lane, on the way to school.

16

Simon's heart started thumping as usual, but not quite as hard as it used to. Lennie looked smaller. Simon felt braver.

'You're pleased to see me, aren't you, Simon? You've got a Mars Bar for me, haven't you, Simon?'

'No.'

Lennie lunged forward and took hold of Simon's bag.

'Get off,' said Simon, pushing at him.

At once, he wished he hadn't. His head was suddenly caught in a painful arm lock, and Lennie was laughing triumphantly.

'Tip!' Simon managed to yell. 'Tip!'

## Chapter Four

A MINUTE LATER, a long tawny shape
streaked along the lane. Lennie saw it first
and let Simon's head go. His eyes were wide,
fixed on the growling creature that was ready
to spring.

'What! Here, don't let him . . . Oi!' he
squealed, trying to back away, but his sleeve
was caught in the strap of Simon's bag.

Simon bent down and took hold of Tip's
collar.

'Easy, Tip,' he said. 'Good dog.' He was
feeling nervous himself. He'd never seen Tip

looking so wild and angry before, his tail
lashing from side to side, his lips drawn back
in a wicked snarl over long, pointed teeth.

'That's not a dog,' panted Lennie,
desperately trying to free his sleeve. 'It's a . . .'

Then Tip opened his big red mouth as wide
as it would go, and roared.

Lennie's face was chalky white, and even though he was free at last, he didn't seem able to run.

'No, he's not a dog,' Simon heard himself say. 'He's a lion. And I've trained him to eat bullies.'

Lennie had begun edging away down the road. A crafty look was coming over his face.

'It's illegal, keeping dangerous animals,' he said, and the colour was creeping back into his face. 'They'll do you for that. You'll do time for that.'

Simon, holding onto Tip's collar, felt the lion's strength under his hands.

'If you tell the police about Tip,' he said calmly, 'I'll get him to track you down. Sniff you out wherever you are. Lions can do that. He'll get you. He's taking a good look at you now. He'll remember you.'

Lennie turned, stumbled, nearly fell, but righted himself and ran away.

Gingerly, Simon patted Tip's head.

'Good . . .' he began. 'I mean, good lion. Come on, let's go home.'

He slipped his scarf through Tip's collar and used it as a lead as he walked him back up the lane, although he knew there was no point. Tip had grown so strong these past few weeks he could have shaken himself free at once if he'd wanted to. He was still only a

cub, but he had a lion's muscles and a lion's
brain.

Mum was running up the lane.

'I heard him roar,' she said. 'I've been a
complete idiot, not facing up to . . . He'll have
to go, Simon. Think of the farmers. Once it gets
out that we've got a lion cub in the house . . .'

'I know, Mum.' Simon felt proud and sad and happy all at the same time. Deep down, he'd known for ages.

'Say good-bye to him then, love. I'll take the morning off work and get onto the safari park right away.'

Simon wanted to get down and put his arms round Tip's neck and have a good cry, but Tip gave a mighty yawn and turned his head away. He looked so noble and lion-like that Simon felt almost shy.

'Bye, Tip,' he said, blinking hard, and was just about to go when the cub put out a forepaw and, with claws sheathed, gently tapped him on the knee.

## Chapter Five

THE FUSS EVERYONE made about Simon
having a lion cub seemed to go on for weeks,
though actually it was only a few days.

The newspapers gave it banner headlines.

WONDER BOY TAMES LION.

'HE WOULDN'T HURT A FLY,' SAYS
SIMON'S MUM.

OUTRAGED FARMERS FEAR FOR LAMBS.

Reporters and photographers cluttered up
the lane and flashbulbs snapped whenever
Simon or his mum showed their faces at
a window.

The police called and asked a lot of questions, especially about Uncle Pete and the man he'd bought the cub from, but Uncle Pete had gone back to sea, and no one knew anything at the dock.

At school, people kept asking Simon questions.

'Did it eat anyone, your lion?'

'Why didn't you set him on Miss Parker?'

'You getting a tiger next?'

After a bit though, the fuss died down.
Things went back to normal, except for Simon.
He had suddenly become quite popular.
People wanted to sit next to him. Girls asked
if they could borrow his crayons. James
wanted to play football with him at break.

But Simon missed Tip all the time. He worried about him, too.

'Maybe the other lions'll bully him,' he said to his mum. 'They might think he's different because he's been brought up by humans.'

He found a book about big cats in the school library and sat for hours looking at it. At night, when he shut his eyes, he imagined himself stepping into one of the pictures.

He would be on a huge plain covered with waving golden grass, dotted about with thorn trees. Every now and then, an ostrich would strut past, or a group of antelope would go leaping off into the distance. And under one of the thorn trees, his massive head crowned by a thick tawny mane, a lion would be lying, his paws stretched out in front of him, his cool eyes scanning the horizon.

'Tip,' Simon would whisper, as he fell asleep. 'Do you remember me?'

# Chapter Six

'NOW LISTEN, EVERYONE,' said Miss Parker one morning.

She waited for silence. It was a long time coming.

'Settle down,' she barked, running out of patience. 'I've got some good news for you. We're going on a class outing.'

'Not another museum,' groaned a girl.

'Can it be to the cinema? Please, Miss!' said another.

'We're going,' said Miss Parker firmly, 'to the safari park.'

There were gasps of excitement.

'Isn't that where your lion is, Simon?'
James said.

Everyone looked at Simon. His heart was
pounding and he was breathing hard, but he
managed not to show it.

'Nah,' he said, coolly. 'Don't know where he
is now.'

The rest of the day crawled past. So did the next, and the next. Simon could not believe that time could pass so slowly.

But at last, the day of the outing came, and the coach pulled away from the school gates. After a century, it turned into the safari park, and after another century, Miss Parker said, 'Now everyone, we're going into the lions' enclosure. Stay in your seats and don't shout or jump around. The driver will go very slowly. You'll all get a good chance to look at the lions.'

Simon felt half-suffocated with excitement as the coach lumbered through the high mesh fence. He looked about him eagerly, but his heart sank. There were too many rocks and bushes here, and the trees were the wrong shape. The grass was too green and the sky dull and cloudy.

It didn't look at all as he had imagined it. It didn't look a bit like Africa. He couldn't believe that Tip was here.

Someone shouted. 'There's one, look!'

'Sshh!' said the others, but they crowded over to the far side of the coach.

Shaking with excitement, Simon pushed his way to the front. But then his heart dropped. The lion was old and tired. His mane was dull and he sat motionless.

That can't be Tip, thought Simon. It isn't Tip!

The coach passed a lioness and a pair of cubs.
'Oo!' cooed everyone. 'Aren't they sweet?'

Simon didn't look at the cubs. His eyes were
hunting everywhere, looking for Tip. But Tip
wasn't there.

Maybe he's dead, Simon thought miserably,
as the gates of the lion enclosure clanged shut
behind the departing coach. Maybe the others
all ganged up on him and killed him.

He managed to wipe his cheeks before
anyone spotted his tears.

# Chapter Seven

'TIME FOR LUNCH,' said Miss Parker
cheerfully, as everyone spilled out of the
coach and headed for the picnic area.

Simon picked up his bag and followed the
others. The picnic area was near the lions'
enclosure, not far from the gates. Simon
wandered towards them.

A car full of old ladies was just about to go
in. A ranger was walking towards the big
gates, ready to open them.

Suddenly Simon had an idea. He dropped
his bag, which he was carrying on his

shoulder, delved into it, and pulled out his
tattered old blue scarf. Trying to look casual,
he strolled across to the car, and bending
down behind it as if he was tying up a
shoelace, he looped the scarf loosely over
the bumper so that one end trailed on
the ground.

'He'll recognise it, I'm sure he will,' he said
to himself. 'Then he'll know I'm here.'

Quickly, he walked back to the picnic area,
took out his lunch box and pretended to eat,
his eyes fixed unwaveringly on the stretch of
enclosure he could see through the double
walls of steel mesh.

'Time to look at the sea-lions,' said Miss
Parker, when everyone had finished eating.
'They're going to feed them soon. That should
be fun.'

'I need the toilet, Miss,' said Simon.
'I'll catch you up.'

'All right,' said Miss Parker. 'Look, the pool's
just down there. You can't get lost. Pick that
wrapper up, Sally, and put it in the bin.
Follow me, everyone!'

The moment they had gone, Simon ran to
the mesh fence and began to walk beside it,
peering inside, searching the enclosure with
his eyes.

Tip! he thought. Where are you? Tip!

Suddenly, he realised that the words were
no longer stuck in his head, but pouring out
of his mouth, for there, just on the other side
of the two mesh fences, was a beautiful
young male lion. He stood with one forepaw
raised, his huge eyes fixed on Simon. And
from his mouth dangled a torn blue scarf.

'Tip! Oh, Tip, it's you!' said Simon, and he

felt sad and happy at the same time so that all he could do was cry.

The lion was pacing up and down along the inside of the fence as if he was looking for a way out.

'Don't, Tip,' said Simon. 'You can't get out.
You've got to stay in here now.'

It was as if Tip understood. He stopped
pacing, then lifting his huge body, he stood

up on his hind legs, stretching his forepaws high and resting them on the fence. Then he opened his red mouth and yawned.

'You're magnificent!' gasped Simon.

Tip dropped down again. He rolled over slowly onto his back and holding the scarf up in his forepaws, he began to play with it exactly as he had done before.

Simon knelt down in the grass to watch him. Then, behind Tip, another lion appeared. Tip rolled onto his feet, and leaving the scarf on the ground, he padded away. He looked back at Simon one more time, then leapt up onto the rock after the other lion and disappeared into the trees.

Simon stood up. He felt different. Taller, stronger, braver. Lion-like. He stretched his arms up as high as they would go and opened his mouth as if in a yawn.

I'm like a lion now, he thought. You'll never get me again, Lennie.

Suddenly, he wanted very much to watch the sea-lions being fed and see the elephants and have a go on the bouncy castle.

Picking up his bag, he began to bound across the grass towards the sea-lions' pool.

# Have you enjoyed this Yellow Banana? There are plenty more to read. Why not try one of these exciting new stories:

### Ghostly Guests *by Penelope Lively*

When the Brown family move to a new house, Marion and Simon discover there are three ghosts already living there! The ghosts make their lives unbearable – how can the children get rid of them?

### Carole's Camel *by Michael Hardcastle*

Carole is left a rather unusual present – a camel called Umberto. It's great to to ride him to school and everyone loves him, even if he is rather smelly. But looking after a real camel can cause a lot of problems. Perhaps she should find him a more suitable home . . .

### The Pony that went to Sea *by K.M. Peyton*

Paddy, an old forgotten pony, is adopted by Tom and Emily Tarboy. One stormy night, Paddy is taken aboard the houseboat where the children live. But during the night the boat breaks free and is carried out to sea. It's up to Paddy to save the day.

### Ollie and the Trainers *by Rachel Anderson*

Ollie has two problems: he has no trainers and he can't read. Dad agrees to buy him some trainers but they turn out to be no ordinary pair. They are Secret Readers and can talk! Can Leftfoot Peter and Rightfoot Paul help Ollie to read?

### Bella's Den *by Berlie Doherty*

Moving to the country, my only friend is Bella. One day she shows me her secret – a den. We go there one night and see some foxes, and in my excitement I blurt out what I've seen and a farmer overhears. He says foxes kill lambs and he's going to hunt them down. I've got to stop him . . .